DISCOVER DOGS WITH THE AMERICAN CANINE ASSOCIATION

I LIKE NEWFOUNDLANDS!

Linda Bozzo

It is the mission of the American Canine Association (ACA) to provide registered dog owners with the educational support needed for raising, training, showing, and breeding the healthiest pets expected by responsible pet owners throughout the world. Through our activities and services, we encourage and support the dog world in order to promote best-known husbandry standards as well as to ensure that the voice and needs of our customers are quickly and properly addressed.

Our continued support, commitment, and direction are guided by our customers, including veterinary, legal, and legislative advisors. ACA aims to provide the most efficient, cooperative, and courteous service to our customers and strives to set the standard for education and problem solving for all who depend on our services.

For more information, please visit www.acacanines.com, email customerservice@acadogs.com, phone 1-800-651-8332, or write to the American Canine Association at PO Box 121107, Clermont, FL 34712.

Published in 2018 by Enslow Publishing, LLC.
101 W. 23rd Street, Suite 240, New York, NY 10011

Library of Congress Cataloging-in-Publication Data

Names: Bozzo, Linda, author.
Title: I like Newfoundlands! / Linda Bozzo.
Description: New York, NY : Enslow Publishing, 2018. | Series: Discover dogs with the American Canine Association | Includes bibliographical references and index. | Audience: Grades K to 3.
Identifiers: LCCN 2017012586| ISBN 9780766091375 (library bound) | ISBN 9780766091351 (pbk.) | ISBN 9780766091368 (6 pack)
Subjects: LCSH: Newfoundland dog—Juvenile literature.
Classification: LCC SF429.N4 B69 2017 | DDC 636.73
LC record available at https://lccn.loc.gov/2017012586

Printed in China

To Our Readers: We have done our best to make sure all websites in this book were active and appropriate when we went to press. However, the author and the publisher have no control over and assume no liability for the material available on those websites or on any websites they may link to. Any comments or suggestions can be sent by email to customerservice@enslow.com.

Photo Credits: Cover, p. 1 dezi/Shutterstock.com; p. 3 (left) Liliya Kulianionak/Shutterstock.com; p. 3 (right) shutternelke/Shutterstock.com; p. 5 Mark Raycroft/Minden Pictures/Getty Images; p. 6 StockImage/Moment/Getty Images; p. 9 cynoclub/iStock/Thinkstock; p. 10 cyran/Shutterstock.com; p. 13 (puppy) Dora Zett/Shutterstock; p. 13 (collar) © graphicphoto/iStock/Thinkstock, (bed) Luisa Leal Photography/Shutterstock.com, (brush) In-Finity/Shutterstock.com, (food and water bowls) exopixel/Shutterstock.com, (leash, toys) © iStockphoto.com/Liliboas; p. 14 Reuters/Alamy Stock Photo; p. 17 Rolf Hicker/All Canada Photos/Getty Images; p. 18 Jeff Haynes/AFP/Getty Images; p. 19 Ermolaev Alexander/Shutterstock.com; p. 21 Dmitry Vinogradov/Shutterstock.com.

Enslow Publishing
101 W. 23rd Street
Suite 240
New York, NY 10011
USA
enslow.com

CONTENTS

IS A NEWFOUNDLAND RIGHT FOR YOU?

Newfoundlands are often called "**Newfies**." They love to swim. If you live near a lake or river, a Newfie might be right for you.

Newfies have webbed feet, like ducks, which make them great swimmers.

A DOG OR A PUPPY?

This giant breed is easy to train. But training takes time. If you do not have time to train a puppy, you may want an older Newfie instead.

Training a Newfoundland should be done early because of its large size.

LOVING YOUR NEWFOUNDLAND

Love your Newfie by cuddling with him. This sweet and patient dog enjoys being with children!

EXERCISE

Newfies need walks on a **leash** to stay fit. You'll want to play games like **fetch** with your dog. Newfies prefer their games in the water.

Until Newfies are done growing, they should have little exercise so their young bones and joints don't get damaged.

FEEDING YOUR NEWFOUNDLAND

Newfies can be fed wet or dry dog food. Ask a **veterinarian (vet)**, a doctor for animals, which food is best for your dog and how much to feed her.

Give your Newfoundland fresh, clean water every day.

Remember to keep your dog's food and water dishes clean. Dirty dishes can make a dog sick.

Do not feed your dog people food. It can make her sick.

Your new dog will need:

a collar with a tag

a bed

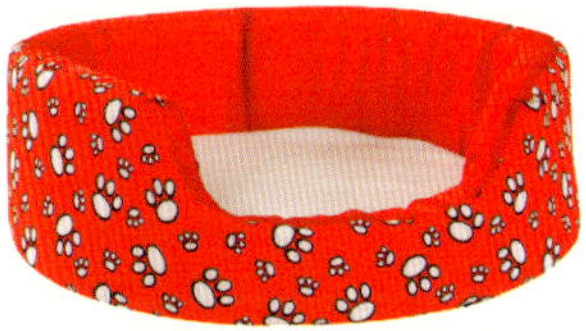

a brush

food and water dishes

a leash

toys

A Newfie's coat has a slightly oily feel to it because it is **water resistant**. This keeps her skin dry and warm in cold water.

GROOMING

Newfies **shed** their thick coat. This means their hair falls out. Your Newfie will need to be brushed and combed often. You can give her baths as needed. Use a special shampoo that is made for dogs.

A Newfie's nails grow fast and will need to be clipped. A vet or **groomer** can show you how. Your dog's ears should be cleaned, and her teeth should be brushed by an adult.

WHAT YOU SHOULD KNOW

Newfies are one of the kindest dogs. They are great with children as well as with other pets. Newfies drool a lot! They are also messy drinkers. Because of a Newfie's heavy coat, this dog needs a cool place to rest.

You will need to take your new dog to the vet for a checkup. He will need shots, called **vaccinations**, and yearly checkups to keep him healthy. If you think your dog may be sick or hurt, call your vet.

A GOOD FRIEND

Newfies are big, lovable friends to all. With lots of care, your Newfie will be the best dog ever!

As a big dog, the Newfie ages more quickly than a small dog. You can expect a Newfie to live around 10 to 12 years.

NOTE TO PARENTS

It is important to consider having your dog spayed or neutered when the dog is young. Spaying and neutering are operations that prevent unwanted puppies and can help improve the overall health of your dog.

It is also a good idea to microchip your dog, in case he or she gets lost. A vet will implant a microchip under the skin containing an identification number that can be scanned at a vet's office or animal shelter. The microchip registry is contacted and the company uses the ID number to look up your information from a database.

Some towns require licenses for dogs, so be sure to check with your town clerk.

For more information, speak with a vet.

There are many dogs, young and old, waiting to be adopted from animal shelters and rescue groups.

Words to Know

fetch To go after a toy and bring it back.

groomer A person who bathes and brushes dogs.

leash A chain or strap that attaches to a dog's collar.

Newfie Another name for a Newfoundland.

shed When dog hair falls out so new hair can grow.

vaccinations Shots that dogs need to stay healthy.

veterinarian (vet) A doctor for animals.

water-resistant Not easily wet.

Read About Dogs

Books

Carney, Elizabeth. *Woof! 100 Fun Facts About Dogs.* Washington, DC: National Geographic Children's Books, 2017.

Morey, Allan. *Newfoundlands* (Big Dogs). North Mankato, MN: Capstone Press, 2016.

Sommer, Nathan. *Newfoundlands* (Awesome Dogs). Minneapolis, MN: Bellwether Media, Inc., 2018.

Websites

American Canine Association Inc., Kids Corner
www.acakids.com
Visit the official website of the American Canine Association.

National Geographic for Kids, Pet Central
kids.nationalgeographic.com/explore/pet-central
Learn more about dogs and other pets at the official site of the National Geographic Society for Kids.

INDEX